# The Frog Principal

By STEPHANIE CALMENSON

Illustrated by DENISE BRUNKUS

Scholastic Press • New York

To Tyler Lew
—S.C.

Gold stars for
Wayne,
Kate the Great,
and Koko the ArtDog
—D.B.

Library of Congress catalog card number: 97-051168

ISBN 0-590-37070-7

10 9 8 7 6 5 4 3          02 03 04 05

Printed in Mexico     49
First edition, August 2001

The text type was set in 16-point Elroy.
The illustrations in this book were rendered
in watercolor and colored pencil.
Book design by Kristina Albertson

**M**r. Bundy is the principal of P.S. 88. His students
and teachers think he's the best principal in town.

One day, Mr. Bundy was at school late planning the next assembly program. He was looking for a special visitor when an ad in the phone book caught his eye. It said:

**MARTY Q. MARVEL, MAGICIAN**
**My MARVEL-ous magic**
**will amaze you!**

"The kids would love a magic show!" thought Mr. Bundy. He called Marty Q. Marvel and asked to see some of his tricks.

In no time, a man wearing a black cape and a magician's hat tripped into Mr. Bundy's office.

"*Whoops!* Marty Q. Marvel here! Allow me to amaze, amuse, and confuse you!" he said.

"May I see some educational tricks, please?" asked Mr. Bundy. "I like my students to learn from our visitors."

"Sure! One math lesson coming right up!" said Marty Q. Marvel. "Watch my hat and tell me how many birds come out."

He began to recite, "And a-one! And a-two! And a-one, two, three! Come out, birds! Fly to me!"

Marty tapped his hat once, twice, three times. No birds.

He turned his hat upside down and shook it hard. Not a feather.

"What kind of
math lesson was that?" asked Mr. Bundy.

"Um, I guess that was my lesson on zero.
Let me try my science lesson. It's on
amphibians."

Before Mr. Bundy could tell the magician
he'd seen enough, Marty was waving his
magic wand in Mr. Bundy's direction, saying,
"He lives in a wood, in a pond, or a bog. He
used to be a principal, but now he's a . . .

. . . FROG!"

**POOF!!!** Mr. Bundy suddenly felt small, strange, and slimy.

"*Ribbit! Ribbit!*" he said.

He cleared his throat, then tried again. Thank goodness real words came out.

"Wh-what have you done to me?" croaked Mr. Bundy.

"*Whoops!* It looks as though I turned you into a frog," said Marty Q. Marvel. "It's amazing. That trick never worked before."

"Kindly *un*-work it," said Mr. Bundy. He was hopping mad.

"I'll check my instruction book," said Marty.

He pulled a rabbit, some flowers, a deck of cards, and a small book out of his bag. He flipped through the book.

"*Buenos días. Muchos gracias. ¿Qué pasa? Whoops!* This is my Spanish dictionary. My instruction book must be at home. I'll be right back," said the magician, tripping out the door.

It was a long night for Mr. Bundy. The sun went down. The sun came up. There was no sign of Marty Q. Marvel.

Finally, Mr. Bundy heard footsteps outside his office. His heart leaped in his little green chest.

"Good morning, Mr. Bundy!" called a voice.

Oh, no! It was Ms. Moore, the vice principal.

"I can't let her see me this way!" thought Mr. Bundy.

He scrawled a note that said:

FAMILY emergency! BE BACK SOON.

Then he hopped from his chair to his desk to the window and out across the school yard.

As he watched his beloved students and teachers go by, Mr. Bundy considered his life as a frog.

"Even though I'm small, green, and slimy, I can still be a good principal, can't I?" he wondered.

He hopped over to a pond to think.

Mr. Bundy's skin was dry, and the water looked awfully good. SPLASH! Mr. Bundy dove in for a swim.

"Wow! These frog legs are amazing!" he thought, kicking around the pond.

A fly whizzed by. Without thinking, Mr. Bundy flicked out his tongue. ZAP! He caught the fly.

"Hmm, not bad," he thought.

At recess, a group of kids came outside to play softball. A girl named Keesha hit the ball, and it went flying!

Roger, Hector, and Nancy all ran after it.

"Uh-oh. I think the ball landed in the pond," said Roger.

"What will we do now?" asked Nancy.

A voice called, "I can help you!"

"Who said that?" asked Hector.

They all thought the voice was coming from the water.

But the next instant a frog jumped out from behind the
cattails and said, "It was me!"

"Huh?" said Roger. "A talking frog?"

"You may consider me an exception to the rule," said Mr. Bundy. "I am a frog. I can talk. And I can get you your ball."

The kids could hardly believe their eyes and ears. Things like this happened only in fairy tales.

"I want one thing in return," continued the frog. "I want to be your principal."

"B-b-but we already have one," said Hector.

"That's right. He's the best!" said Nancy.

That made Mr. Bundy proud. He wanted to continue being their principal—even if he was a frog.

"It's up to you," said Mr. Bundy. "I will get the ball, but only if I can be your principal."

The kids went off to talk it over.

"He can't be our principal," said Roger. "He's a frog."

"We can tell him he can be our principal, but we don't have to mean it," said Nancy.

"I guess it's the only way to get our ball back," said Hector.

So the kids told the frog it would be okay.

"Do you promise?" asked Mr. Bundy.

"We promise," said the kids, crossing their fingers behind them.

Mr. Bundy hopped into the pond and got the ball. He tossed it to the kids.

"Thanks, frog!" they called, running back to school.

"Wait for me!" cried Mr. Bundy. "I can't go that fast!"

But the kids were already too far away to hear him.

That afternoon, Ms. Moore held a special assembly.

"Mr. Bundy has been called away," she told the students.
"While he's gone, we must work together to . . ."

*Knock, knock.*

"Roger, please see who that is," said Ms. Moore.

Roger was pretty sure he knew who it was. He walked to
the door and opened it a crack.

"Let me in!" croaked a voice.

Roger slammed the door and returned to his seat.

"Who was there, Roger?" asked Ms. Moore. "You look as though you've seen a ghost."

"It's not a ghost, it's a frog!" called Alice, a kindergarten student. By now, half the school had heard about the talking frog, and Alice had a habit of telling the truth, no matter what.

"Will someone please tell me what's going on?" asked Ms. Moore.

The kids told her the whole story.

"We promised the frog he could be our principal," said Roger.

Ms. Moore thought her students were joking. She couldn't wait to see what they were up to.

"A promise is a promise," she said. "If you promised the frog he could be your principal, you have to let him in."

Roger opened the door. Mr. Bundy, the frog principal, walked down the aisle and up to the stage.

Poor Ms. Moore almost fainted.

"*Ribbit* . . . er . . . good afternoon," croaked the frog. "I've heard that Mr. Bundy is a very good principal. I will do my best to fill his shoes while he is gone. Of course, they may be a little large for me. Ha, ha!"

No one else laughed. They were too stunned.

"It must be a computer trick," whispered one of the teachers.

"It will be business as usual until Mr. Bundy returns," continued the frog principal. "In fact, you may call me Mr. B."

After the assembly, Mr. B made school rounds, hopping up and down the halls. He was almost trampled by two students racing by.

"No running in the halls, please!" called Mr. Bundy.

The students, Keesha and Max, stopped and looked around.

"I'm down here!" Mr. B reminded them.

Max looked down. "This is so weird," he whispered to Keesha.

"No kidding," said Keesha. "We almost squished our principal!"

In the gym, the kids were playing leapfrog. Mr. Bundy couldn't resist. He hopped in, leaped over Hector's shoulders, then hopped back out.

"Please tell me that didn't happen," said Hector, rolling his eyes.

The kindergarten class was learning about water when Mr. B showed up.

"Hello, Mr. B!" called the students.

"Hi, everyone!" answered Mr. Bundy.

The next thing they knew—SPLASH!—their principal was swimming laps in the sink. They tried their best not to giggle.

"Very refreshing," said Mr. Bundy.

"Here, Mr. B," said Alice. She handed him a paper towel to dry off with.

"Thank you very much," said Mr. Bundy. He went out, leaving a trail of small puddles behind him.

Mr. Bundy went to Ms. Brown's science class next.
Nancy had a shoe box with holes in the top.

"What have you got there?" asked Mr. Bundy.

Nancy opened the box to show him. ZAP! ZAP! ZAP!
Mr. Bundy swallowed Nancy's bug collection.

"The principal ate my homework!" cried Nancy.

"Ms. Brown, please give this student a gold star!"
said Mr. Bundy. "Her collection of bugs was delicious . . .
I mean, excellent."

As the weeks passed, Mr. Bundy tried to be the best frog principal he could be. The students tried their best to accept him. But it was hard. They were sorry they had lied.

"We shouldn't have made a promise if we didn't mean it," said Roger.

"It's embarrassing having a frog for a principal," said Hector. "But I guess we deserve it."

"I want Mr. Bundy back!" said Nancy.

Mr. Bundy heard his students and his heart sank. He kept calling Marty Q. Marvel, but there was no answer. He prayed the magician would come back.

"If not, I'll be a frog forever and ever," he thought.

Then one day at recess, Mr. B was watching a softball game from his office. He was wondering how long he could go on being a frog principal when suddenly. . .

. . . a ball came flying through the window. It landed with a thump on Mr. B's little green head. Stars were spinning in his eyes.

Out of nowhere, Mr. Bundy started reciting a magic spell. "And a-one! And a-two! And a-one, two, three! Look who's back! Hooray! It's . . .

. . . ME!"

POOF! Mr. Bundy was his old self again.

Ms. Moore heard the commotion and came running.

"Mr. Bundy! Welcome back!" she cried. "I was so worried about you. Is everything all right?"

Mr. Bundy looked down. He saw his own two hands. He saw his own two legs.

"Everything's great!" he said.

"You won't believe who our substitute principal
was," said Ms. Moore. "I'll let the children tell you
all about him."

Mr. Bundy went to the window and waved. The
students cheered wildly and were so excited to
have their principal back that no one even
noticed when . . .

. . . **ZAP!**

Mr. Bundy swallowed a fly.